The Alden Family Mysteries
by Gertrude Chandler Warner

THE BOXCAR CHILDREN
SURPRISE ISLAND
THE YELLOW HOUSE MYSTERY
MYSTERY RANCH
MIKE'S MYSTERY
BLUE BAY MYSTERY
THE WOODSHED MYSTERY
THE LIGHTHOUSE MYSTERY
MOUNTAIN TOP MYSTERY
SCHOOLHOUSE MYSTERY
CABOOSE MYSTERY
HOUSEBOAT MYSTERY
SNOWBOUND MYSTERY
TREE HOUSE MYSTERY
BICYCLE MYSTERY
MYSTERY IN THE SAND
MYSTERY BEHIND THE WALL
BUS STATION MYSTERY
BENNY UNCOVERS A MYSTERY

CABOOSE MYSTERY

GERTRUDE CHANDLER WARNER

Illustrated by David Cunningham

ALBERT WHITMAN & Company
Niles, Illinois

To My Readers

The Little North Railroad is a storybook railroad, but the cabooses are real cabooses. With the help of six very kind trainmen, I myself took a trip by caboose, riding on the back platform and feeling just like Benny. I ran the Diesel engine, blew the whistle, rang the bell, and watched as the trainmen set off dynamite on the track, just as it says in these pages. As for the story, the adventures are wholly imaginary.

GERTRUDE CHANDLER WARNER

ISBN 0-8075-1009-2

Published simultaneously in Canada by General Publishing, Limited, Toronto.

7 9 10 8

Printed in the U.S.A.

Contents

CHAPTER 1

Grandfather's Idea

One morning Benny Alden sat in his room thinking. The four Alden children lived with their grandfather, James Alden.

"What a lot of adventures we have had," thought Benny. "First we lived in a boxcar in the woods. That was fun! Then after we found Grandfather, we have been to so many places and had so many surprises. By the way—"

Benny had a sudden thought. He ran downstairs as fast as he could. He found his grandfather at his desk. Violet was nearby, sewing on a button.

Benny said, "Grandfather, I just remembered you had a plan for this summer!"

Jessie walked in. "Yes, you did," she said. "And then we suddenly went away and found the mystery in the schoolhouse."

Henry appeared at the door. "And that spoiled your plan, Grandfather," he said.

"Oh, no," said Mr. Alden. "It didn't spoil my plan at all. We can still go on this trip if you want to."

"Of course we want to!" said Violet. "You always have such wonderful ideas."

"Come and sit under the trees," said Mr. Alden, "and I'll tell you all about it. Thank you, my dear, for sewing on my button." He put on his coat.

Watch, the dog, trotted along with Jessie. He lay down on her feet.

Grandfather began, "You see I have a friend who owns a railroad."

"A railroad!" said Benny.

Mr. Alden smiled. "Yes, it is called the Little North Railroad. Sometimes my friend lets people rent an old-fashioned wooden caboose. It is put on the end of a freight train and travels along with the train. So I thought we could take a trip in a caboose."

"What a neat idea!" said Benny. "I never saw the inside of a caboose."

"Neither did I," said Mr. Alden, smiling.

Henry said, "That would be an adventure for sure. Where could we go?"

"Anywhere the Little North Railroad goes."

Violet asked, "Have you really rented a caboose, Grandfather?"

"Yes, my dear, I have rented two." His eyes twinkled. "I was sure one of you would remember my plan. We can have two cabooses, one for the girls, and one for Henry, Benny, and me."

"And we can get together for meals," said Benny.

Henry laughed at his younger brother. "Always thinking of something to eat, Ben," he said.

"I like to eat," said Benny. "Do we do our own cooking?"

"Yes," said Mr. Alden. "That will be part of the fun. Every caboose has a few pans and dishes in it. There is always a stove and a sink, and an icebox, too. You may want to buy more dishes, Jessie. You are the housekeeper."

"Oh, I'd rather use the caboose dishes. It would be fun to try," said Jessie. "Why can't we drive down to the freightyard now? We can see for ourselves what a caboose is like."

"Just what I planned," said Grandfather, getting up.

Henry got out the station wagon. Everyone climbed in.

Benny saw the two cabooses first. He said, "Oh, they are not just alike! One is big and one is little."

"There must be some reason," said Grandfather. "Just look at the new red paint on the big one! We'll soon find out."

The conductor was on the steps of the small caboose. When he saw the family coming, he smiled and got off the train to meet them. He said, "Good morning. You must be the Aldens. My name is Carr."

Benny said, "That's neat! Your name is Carr, and you take care of cars."

"That's right. I hear plenty of jokes about my name."

Mr. Alden said, "My granddaughters, Jessie and

Violet, want to see where they are going to keep house."

"Fine!" said Mr. Carr. "Climb right in and look around all you like. I want to tell you, Mr. Alden, that the big caboose hasn't been used lately. It had to

be painted. But I thought it would be better for you because the windows are much bigger. You can sit by the window and read. That big caboose has some history, but you'll hear about that later."

As they went up the steps of the small caboose, Benny said in a low voice to his brother, "Did Mr. Carr say history or mystery?"

"He said history," said Henry, laughing. "But I'm sure you'll think there is a mystery, too."

"No," said Benny. "I don't need a mystery. Just traveling in a caboose is good enough for me."

The Aldens began to look around. Jessie opened the icebox.

Mr. Carr said, "You see it is small. We stop often for ice and water. But you will have to take canned food with you. Then sometimes we stop on a siding for an hour or two, and you can go shopping."

Henry took the cover off the little stove and looked in. He said, "This seems to run on bottled gas."

"Right," said Mr. Carr. "If you are cold, light the stove. You'll get a little heat."

"I shouldn't think it would get very cold in August," said Henry.

"Well, it does. But there are plenty of blankets. There are sheets and towels, too. And see, the beds are bunks."

"Oh, boy, I'd like the top bunk!" said Benny.

"You can have it," said Henry, laughing. "I'd rather have the lower one, anyway."

Grandfather said, "Look! The mattresses are covered with old black leather. My friend asked me if I wanted new covers, and I said no. I thought you'd all like the caboose just as it always was."

Then the Aldens went across from the little caboose to the big one.

But Benny went right through to the back platform. He said, "Oh, this is just the place for me! There is room for three. This is where I shall sit on the very end of the train and watch the country go flying by!"

Mr. Carr laughed. He said, "When do you want to go, Mr. Alden? I have a short freight that leaves tomorrow. I'm going on that one myself. Then there is another going the next day."

Everyone looked at Benny. He said just what they knew he would. "Let's go tomorrow!"

Grandfather smiled at Mr. Carr. He said, "My family likes to move fast. We'll start tomorrow."

"Be here before one o'clock, then," Mr. Carr said. "Be sure to bring everything you need."

The Aldens walked back to the station wagon. Jessie was already making a list of canned food to buy.

Suddenly Benny said, "The big caboose was quite different. Did you notice?"

"Yes, it was much better," said Grandfather. "The floor was better, and the walls were better."

Benny said, "Did you notice that the walls looked as if some fancy wood had been taken off? And there were curtain rods on the windows, but no curtains."

Henry said, "Of course it looked new because it had just been painted red."

But Benny had begun to wonder. The last thing he said when he went to bed was, "That big caboose has a history. Maybe it has a mystery, too."

CHAPTER 2

All Aboard!

What a rush! Next day the Aldens went dashing around buying food and packing their things. By noon they were ready to go. When they were leaving, Watch, the dog, trotted along with Jessie. He was ready to go, too.

"You can't come, old boy," said Henry. "Too bad. You wouldn't like riding in a caboose."

Jessie tried to explain to Watch why he couldn't go. At last she thought he understood. Anyway he did not whine. He turned right around and went back into the house where Mrs. McGregor, the housekeeper, was waiting for him.

Very soon Henry had parked the station wagon in the freightyard with the trainmen's cars. He planned to leave it for Mr. Carter, who worked for Mr. Alden. Then everyone helped move into the two cabooses.

"Oh, what fun this is!" said Jessie. She and Violet began to put the cans of food on the shelves in the big caboose. Henry and Benny poured water into the tank and lifted a big cake of ice into the icebox.

When the things were put away, the family got out again. They stood by the steps and watched the engineer far down the tracks.

"Look, Grandfather," said Benny. "There's a postman! Do you suppose he would have any mail for you?"

"Well, perhaps I might have a letter from my friend who owns the Little North Railroad," said Mr. Alden. "He knows we'll be on this freight. But I never knew a postman delivered mail to a freight train before. If I have any, Mr. Carr will bring it to me."

"I'll run down and see," said Benny. He was off before they could stop him.

"I'd better go with him," said Henry. And off he went, too. He caught up with Benny, and they reached Mr. Carr and the postman at the same time.

The postman was a very tall, heavy man. His blue-gray uniform and cap were too small for him. He had

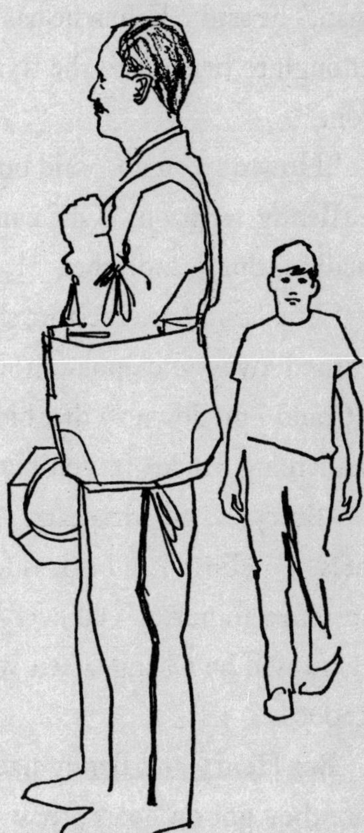

a small black mustache and black eyes. He looked at the two boys closely.

Benny said, "I didn't know a postman came to a freight train, Mr. Carr."

Mr. Carr laughed. "This is a very special postman," he said. "When he has a letter for me, he is kind enough to bring it to the train. His name is Sid Weston."

"How do you do," said both boys.

Benny went on. "Our name is Alden. Is there any mail for our grandfather, Mr. Alden?"

"No," said Mr. Weston, shaking his head. Then he turned away and spoke in a low voice to Mr. Carr. "Could I go down to that big caboose and just look at something inside? It won't take ten minutes."

"Sorry," said Mr. Carr. "We can't wait ten minutes. You boys run back as fast as you can. We go in just two minutes. Tell everyone to sit down because there will be a bang when we back the train into the caboose."

But Henry and Benny had already gone. The minute they got on board, they waved back to Mr. Carr.

Mr. Carr raised his arm and waved at the engineer. The freight train backed toward the caboose. Then came the bang! The little caboose and the big caboose were coupled at the very end of the train, behind the caboose used by the trainmen.

"What a train!" said Grandfather. "Three cabooses in a row! People will smile when this Little North freight goes by."

The Aldens heard the whistle on the engine far ahead. Then very slowly the train began to move. Mr. Carr swung himself onto a boxcar.

"Say, isn't this exciting!" said Benny. "To be riding in a caboose at last. I've always wanted to live in a caboose."

"So have I," said Grandfather, smiling.

"Come on, Ben," said Henry. "Let's sit out on the back platform. Want to come, Jessie?"

"Yes, I'd like to," said Jessie.

Violet said, "I'll stay with Grandfather in the big caboose."

"Isn't this great, flying along!" said Benny after a few minutes. Then he leaned forward and said,

"Henry, did you really look at that big postman? Did you hear him ask to see this caboose?"

"Yes, Ben, I did," said Henry. He looked quickly at Benny. "I thought it was a strange thing to ask."

"Well, I thought it was an awfully strange thing to ask," said Benny.

Jessie said, "What are you boys talking about?"

Henry told her about Sid Weston, the postman. She said, "What do you think he wanted to look at?"

"I haven't any idea," said Henry. "He was a very heavy man. I'm sure he couldn't have run as fast as we did."

"Yes, wasn't he enormous?" said Benny.

"Even his cap was too small for him," said Henry, laughing.

"A mystery!" shouted Benny. "The mysterious caboose!"

"Now don't get excited, Benny," said Jessie. "It is probably something very simple. Maybe he is just interested in trains. Some people are."

But Benny had the last word as usual. "That postman certainly thought there was something different about this big caboose, and sometime I'll find out. You just wait and see."

"Right!" said Henry. "You didn't hear the postman, Jessie. I'm sure he was worried about something."

"I'm sure you're right if you both say so," said Jessie. "But let's enjoy this lovely country with all the woods and fields."

"I'm enjoying them," said Benny. "I noticed every cornfield we passed. The corn ought to be ripe soon."

Along went the train. It passed through one small town after another. Just before five o'clock Benny said, "Look at that ladder over our heads. I'd like to climb up and walk on top of the caboose."

Just as he said this, a foot suddenly appeared on the top step of the ladder. Then another foot appeared, then two long legs dressed in overalls.

"Oh, look what's coming!" said Benny.

At last a head appeared with a railroad cap, and a smiling man said, "Hello! I hope I didn't scare you?"

"No," said Henry. "But you surprised us."

"I have a message from the engineer," said the man.

Benny said, "He's the boss of the train."

"No," said the man, shaking his head. "The conductor, Mr. Carr, is the boss of the train. The engineer is number-two man. I'm the brakeman. My name is Al."

"I never knew the conductor was the boss," said Benny.

"Well, he is," said Al. "The engineer, Mr. Davis, runs the train, but the conductor tells him when to stop and when to go."

"What's this message, Al?" asked Henry.

The brakeman seemed to be right at home on the ladder. He held on with one hand, swung one foot, and took his cap off and put it on again. He said, "Really I have two messages. The first one is this. If you are in any trouble, you will want to stop the train."

Benny said, "Oh, I don't think we will have any trouble."

"You never can tell, Ben," said Henry. "What do we do, Al?"

"Well, there's a little lever by the desk. You turn

that halfway. That puts on the air brakes. Even if we had a hundred cars, the train would stop."

"I'll look for that lever when we go inside," said Henry.

Violet came to the door to see what was going on. She was just in time to hear Benny say, "Al, did you see that big postman just before we started? Did you hear what he said?"

"I saw him," said Al. "But I didn't hear what he said. Why?"

"Oh, nothing," said Benny.

"I have another message," said Al. "At about five o'clock we go right through the engineer's field of corn. He has sweet corn on both sides of the tracks. Mr. Davis says if you want some corn for supper, just get off and pick all you want."

"Sweet corn!" said Violet. "We love it. This will certainly be fresh."

"Cook it as soon as you pick it," said Al. "I'm getting enough for our supper, too."

"Oh, are you the cook?" Jessie asked.

"Yes," said Al, "I do the cooking. I'd ask you to

come into our caboose, but Mr. Carr wants the door locked at the end of your second caboose. He thinks you'll be better off that way. We use our caboose just for work, you know."

"I'll put the water on to boil right now," said Jessie. "Then it will be ready for the corn."

"Oh, don't do that, miss," said Al. "Get a big kettle of cold water and put in the corn. When the water is boiling fast, the corn is done."

"Thank you," said Jessie, "I'll try it."

"It's the best way to cook corn," Al told her. "I'll stay right here, and you get off when I do."

Jessie went in to fill the biggest kettle with cold water. She told Mr. Alden what they were going to do. Everyone stood ready to get off. Soon the train began to slow down.

"I see the cornfield!" Benny called out. "How many ears shall we pick, Jessie?"

"Oh, I should say two dozen ears. Put them in this old box."

The train stopped, and everyone got off and began to pick corn.

Mr. Alden said, "I haven't picked corn for years. What else are we going to have for supper?"

Jessie answered, "Plenty of butter on the corn, hamburgers, cookies, and milk."

"Good enough," said Grandfather. "I'm hungry already."

The engineer gave a loud whistle, and they all climbed back into the caboose. Everyone sat down and helped pull off the corn husks. Jessie dropped the ears into the cold water, and Henry turned on the stove.

Soon they were sitting down to supper.

"What delicious corn!" said Mr. Alden.

"It certainly is fresh," said Benny. "Right from the field into the kettle!"

After the dishes were done, the Aldens took turns riding on the little back platform. As they sat there, Al came climbing down the ladder again.

He said, "Mr. Carr forgot to tell you that we stop at Beaver Lake at nine o'clock tomorrow morning. You will like that."

"Why?" asked Benny.

"You always want to know why, don't you? Well, you can watch real live beavers at work. We have to stop for an hour to load freight, and you might as well watch something interesting."

"I should think the beavers would run away if they saw us watching them," said Benny.

"That's the secret," said Al. "They won't see you. Now don't ask me why, young man. Just wait and see. One more thing. There is an old man who takes care of these wild beavers. He's a strange old fellow, but he doesn't want people to kill all the beavers. So he lives in the woods and keeps the hunters away. You may see Old Beaver, and you may not. He's odd. Then a little later we stop at Pinedale for ice and water."

"Thanks a lot," said Mr. Alden. Al disappeared up the ladder.

When the stars came out, Mr. Alden said, "Our lights are not bright enough to read by. I'm going to bed."

"I'm tired, too," said Violet. The girls said good-night and went into the small caboose.

Henry and Grandfather put clean sheets on the three old black mattresses, and Benny started to climb into his top bunk in the lookout. He began to laugh.

"I can hardly reach these steps with my feet," he said. "First one side and then the other. I guess these footholds were made for a man."

Mr. Alden and Henry watched.

"Just made it, Ben," said Henry. "Those steps are too hard for you."

"But I like it up here," said Benny. "I can look out at the stars."

He began to wonder about the postman and the beavers and the big caboose, but suddenly he fell asleep.

The caboose rattled and banged along until morning.

CHAPTER 3

Beaver Man

The train did not stop during the night. Once Benny said loudly, "I'll tell you in the morning!"

"Morning?" Grandfather said. He woke up suddenly. "Is it morning?"

Henry whispered, "No, Grandfather. Benny's talking in his sleep."

When it was really morning, Benny said, "I didn't sleep a wink last night."

Henry laughed. He said, "Oh, no?"

"No, I didn't," said Benny again. "But you and Grandfather did. I heard you both snoring all night."

"I'm sorry I kept you awake, Benny," said Mr. Alden. He winked at Henry. "I know I do snore."

"I could go right back to sleep," Benny said.

"Oh, don't do that, Benny," called Violet. "You'll miss the beavers. Remember we get off at Beaver Lake at nine o'clock."

"That's right," agreed Benny. "I do want to see the beavers. I guess I can stay awake that long."

After breakfast, Benny said, "I'm going to sit on the back platform until nine o'clock."

His two sisters went with him this time. The train went through many small places without stopping. The Aldens waved at everyone they saw.

Suddenly Benny said, "Jessie, did you notice the workmen at the last station we passed? They pointed at our big caboose and began to laugh."

"Yes," said Jessie. "I suppose we do look funny, with three cabooses in a row."

"But not that funny," said Benny. "I'm sure they were pointing at the big caboose and at us."

Violet said, "I don't think they are pointing at us. They point to something on the caboose."

"Right over our heads, Violet," said Benny. "Maybe there is something on the caboose."

They looked up, but all they could see was the number of the car, 777.

Soon they heard Mr. Carr call out, "Beaver Lake, Beaver Lake!"

They were all ready to jump down when the train stopped. Mr. Carr and Al met them at the steps.

Benny said, "Oh, I wanted to ask you about the big caboose. You said it had a history."

Mr. Carr laughed and said, "So I did. But I haven't time now. I can't even go with you. I have to watch the men unload the freight. But Al can go with you."

Al led the way. A small river went under the railroad track. They followed it. Soon they reached some thick woods. Al took them along a path. They could not see the river, but they could hear it rushing along.

Al pointed to a sign that said "Beaver Lake." "You could go on alone," he said, "but I like to watch the beavers myself."

Benny said, "I suppose Old Beaver put up that sign?"

"That's right," said Al. "Sometimes he will come and talk. Sometimes not. This is the place where I usually meet him."

But no one was there.

Soon there was another sign. It said "Please do not talk."

Not even Benny said a word after that.

Then the Aldens saw something that looked like a tent. It had a long bench inside. The roof and one wall of the tent were made to look like real bushes. A sign said, "Sit down and watch. Room for six only."

Everyone had the same thought—how lucky! There were exactly six people, counting Al.

The Aldens could look out through holes in the bushes and see the river, only now the river was a lake. Al pointed. Then everyone saw a big beaver.

The beaver was swimming along with only his head showing. When the beaver came to the round roof of his house, he stopped. Then he began to climb up. Benny noticed that the beaver was covered with mud. Soon he saw why.

The beaver climbed to the top of his house. Then he slid down and scraped off the mud. After that, the beaver climbed up the other side of the house and slapped the mud down with his tail. Then the Aldens knew that the beaver meant to do this.

Suddenly there was a loud crash in the bushes, and a tree fell with a splash into the water. Beside the stump was another beaver. It had cut the little tree down by gnawing the trunk with its sharp teeth.

The Aldens could not take their eyes off this beaver. It walked along the tree it had just cut down. Then it began to gnaw the tree in two, exactly in the middle.

Part of the tree fell into the water. When the tree was cut into two pieces, the beaver swam out and pushed the two parts together, side by side. Then he pushed them both down the lake to the dam. They were just the right length and stayed on top of the dam to keep water from spilling over.

Just then Al looked at his watch and got up to go. The rest followed. They were near the first sign when they heard something in the bushes.

"Hello, folks," said a deep voice. They all turned around.

"Yes, I'm Old Beaver," said the man. He had thick gray hair, and his face was almost covered with a curly gray beard. He was smiling.

Grandfather said, "You are doing a fine job saving a few beavers. They are wonderful animals."

"Thank you," said Old Beaver. "They are smarter

than we are in some ways. May I ask how you got here?"

Grandfather laughed. "We came on the caboose of a freight train. We are having a new kind of vacation."

"This young man seems to be having a good time," said Old Beaver, looking at Benny.

Benny said, "Yes, I'm having a grand time. We cook and eat and sleep in the caboose. It's Number 777."

"What?" said Old Beaver. "Number 777?" He suddenly turned around and crashed into the woods without another word.

"What do you know!" cried Benny, staring.

"Well, what's the matter with him?" asked Henry.

"Come on," said Al. "He's always been odd. We can't bother with him."

Grandfather said, "I should say he was odd."

When the Aldens reached the station, they looked all over the outside of the caboose. They could not see anything strange. All they could see was the number, 777.

Violet said softly, "But Number 777 was enough to scare Old Beaver."

When the train had started again, Mr. Alden said, "Al told us that the next station will be Pinedale. We get off there to get ice and water. Maybe someone can tell us at Pinedale about Old Beaver. And maybe they will know what is so strange about our caboose, Number 777."

CHAPTER 4

A Strange Tale

Very soon the train slowed down at Pinedale and stopped. Six men were standing on the platform. Some of them were laughing and pointing as the Aldens got off the caboose.

Benny went up to a tall man and said, "We'd like to know what is different about our caboose. Why are the men pointing at it?"

"That's easy, sonny," said the man, laughing. "That caboose is the famous old Number 777. It used to be white with gold numbers. It's a circus caboose!"

The Aldens stared at the man. A circus caboose! So this might have something to do with history and mystery!

The tall man smiled. "You're surprised, aren't you? I can tell you a lot more about your caboose. My name is Shaw. I'm the stationmaster."

"I'm glad to meet you," said Grandfather. "My name is Alden. My grandchildren are very much interested in anything you may say about our caboose."

Just then the Aldens noticed that one of the station workmen had walked over to the big caboose. He was standing there looking at it with his head on one side. He had his hands on his hips. He wore a funny, small hat and big shoes turned up at the toes. But there was something sad about his face.

Mr. Shaw called to the workman and said, "How about it? What do you think of Number 777 in its new red dress?"

The workman drawled, "It couldn't fool us! We'd know that caboose if we saw it in China!"

Everyone began to laugh. Nobody could help laughing. There was something about this man that was very funny. And this was strange, too, because the man looked sad.

Suddenly the workman said to Henry, "I'll get you

the ice and water that you need."

The man turned and left quickly.

Henry started to say no, but Mr. Shaw said out of the side of his mouth, "Let him do it. I'll tell you why later."

When the workman was out of sight, Mr. Shaw said, "It will do that man good to help you. He hardly ever says a word. I was surprised when he offered to help you."

Benny said, "Mr. Shaw, it's funny about that man. He looks so sad, and yet he makes me laugh just to look at him. He ought to be a clown."

"He was a clown," said Mr. Shaw. "How did you ever guess? He was called Cho-Cho, and he traveled with a circus. He used to live in Pinedale before he joined the circus. That's why we all know caboose Number 777. Cho-Cho was always on the circus train."

"Was that a long time ago?" asked Henry.

"Yes, quite a few years ago. That circus train came this way every summer. It used the tracks of the Little North Railroad. We trainmen got to know a lot of these circus people. We saw them every year. Some of us even went to see the show in the nearest big town."

"Why is Cho-Cho so sad now?" asked Benny.

"That's quite a story," said Mr. Shaw. "His wife was Chi-Chi, the high-wire artist. Her whole family was famous. Her mother was so wonderful that some king or other in Europe gave her a beautiful diamond necklace. When her mother grew old, she gave the necklace to Chi-Chi. I remember when it came. Chi-Chi showed it to everyone right on this very platform. She loved to show it because it was so beautiful. But she never wore it when she was doing tricks. She wore a cheap copy that sparkled. Then one night she fell. She slipped on the wire and was instantly killed."

"How awful!" said Jessie and Violet.

"Yes, it was a terrible thing. It was awful for Cho-Cho. He left the circus and came to live in Pinedale again. He soon ran out of money, so he agreed to work for me around the station. He had to sell his talking horse, too."

"Talking horse?" asked Benny.

Another man spoke up. "Yes, sir! That was a beautiful horse—a special color. Never saw a horse like him. He had four white feet and a white star on his forehead. His coat was golden brown."

"That's right," said Mr. Shaw. "His tail was cream color and wavy, and it was so long it almost touched the ground."

"He sounds wonderful," said Violet. "How did he talk?"

"Cho-Cho asked him questions. He tossed his head for yes and shook it for no. Then he would paw with his foot to answer number questions. If Cho-Cho asked him how many were two and one, the horse pawed three times. At the end of the act, Cho-Cho always said, 'What do you want to do now, Major?' and the horse would lie down and shut his eyes."

"What a pity he had to sell that horse," said Grandfather. "Do you know who bought him?"

"Oh, yes. A man named John Cutler bought him to amuse his children. The Cutlers live in Glass Factory Junction. That is the next station. They live about a mile from the station through the woods."

"Oh, I'd love to see that horse," said Benny.

"Well, you can. If you can walk a mile and back."

Mr. Alden said, "If Cho-Cho owned the diamond necklace, I don't see why he didn't sell it. Maybe he could have kept the horse."

"Oh, the necklace was lost," said Mr. Shaw. "Chi-Chi always hid it when she wasn't wearing it. She would never tell anyone where it was, not even Cho-Cho."

Benny shouted, "Maybe she hid it in our caboose!"

"No, not likely," said Mr. Shaw. "The police looked through every car in that circus train, but they never found it. Anyway, Chi-Chi never lived in that caboose."

Another man said, "She spent a lot of time there, though."

"Yes, she did," agreed Mr. Shaw. "The owner's wife lived in Number 777, and she made a great friend of Chi-Chi. They fixed up that caboose with lace curtains and everything. Look! Here comes Cho-Cho. See if you can get him to tell you the rest. It will do him good to talk."

The Aldens watched Cho-Cho as he came back with two pails of water and ice on a truck.

Before anyone could stop Benny, he ran up to the old clown.

"Mr. Cho-Cho," Benny said, "Mr. Shaw has been telling us about you. He told us about your wife's diamond necklace. Do you think someone could have stolen it?"

For a minute Cho-Cho did not say anything. It looked as if he were going to turn and run away. Then he said in almost a whisper, "Yes, boy, I think the Thin Man stole it."

"And who was the Thin Man?" asked Henry.

"He was my friend. He had a sideshow in the circus with me."

"What makes you think he stole the diamonds?" asked Henry.

"Well, one day Chi-Chi was showing the diamonds to everybody. I saw her give them to the Thin Man, but I never saw him give them back. He said he did, but Chi-Chi was dead then, and nobody else saw anything at all. At first I believed my friend."

"Did you get the police?" asked Benny.

"Oh, yes. We had a terrible time! Everybody was upset. The police believed that the Thin Man stole the necklace. And at last I believed it myself."

"Why?" asked Benny.

"The next day the Thin Man disappeared."

Mr. Alden nodded. "That does look bad for poor Mr. Thin Man."

Jessie said, "I should think it would be easy for the police to find him if he were really very thin."

"Oh, he was thin, all right! You could see his bones. He had a long black beard down to his waist."

"Of course he could cut that off," said Henry.

"Yes, that is the first thing he would do. The police had men on the lookout for miles and miles. But nobody ever found a single sign of the Thin Man."

Mr. Shaw said, "Let me tell them about the Thin Man's best friend. He lives at Beaver Lake. He was so angry at everybody that he can't bear to hear anything about Number 777, even to this day. He's an odd fellow and is taking care of some wild beavers at Beaver Lake."

"Oh, oh! We know him," shouted Benny. "And he was really angry when he heard we came from Number 777."

Mr. Shaw nodded. "He would be. The people in that caboose made his best friend run away. Old Beaver never believed that the Thin Man stole the diamonds."

"Here's another thing," said Henry. "Do you know anything about a big postman named Sid Weston who came to this train with a letter for Mr. Carr?"

"No, I never heard of him. Why?"

"Well, he wanted to look around in our big caboose, but Mr. Carr said there wasn't time. Why do you suppose he wanted to do that?"

Cho-Cho threw his hands up in the air. "Maybe he is interested in trains. Lots of people come to take pictures of the cars on this old railroad."

Benny said, "I want to see your horse, Cho-Cho, if he is at Glass Factory Junction."

"I'm sorry, Benny. We can't take time," said Grandfather. "We want to see the glass."

Benny said, "But I'd rather see the talking horse."

Jessie said, "Oh, Benny, glassmaking is so interesting. You never saw anyone blow glass, did you?"

"No," said Benny, "and I never saw a talking horse either."

Mr. Shaw laughed. "You girls will like the glass. There are pieces of broken glass all over the place. You can pick them up and have them polished."

"What colors are they?" asked Violet.

"Every color, and some are mixed colors. You can find red and white ones, black and white, and all shades of blue and green. The pieces make beautiful pins and bracelets."

Henry and the clown put the ice and water in the two cabooses. As Mr. Alden started to get on the train, Mr. Shaw whispered, "I'm certainly amazed. I never heard Cho-Cho talk so much in my whole life. He never says a word if he can help it."

"This time he couldn't help it," said Benny, laughing.

CHAPTER 5

Glass Factory Junction

In a short time the train stopped at Glass Factory Junction. The Aldens got off the train and looked around. They could not see any sign of a town. There was a small freight station on one side of the tracks and a large factory on the other. Everything seemed to be in the middle of the woods. Trees grew almost down to the tracks.

"I wonder where the town is," said Benny.

Al came to meet them. "The town is on the other side of the woods," he said. "It's a very small town, anyway. But we have to stop here just the same to unload potash for the factory. And this glass is all over the ground." He picked up a blue piece.

"Isn't that beautiful!" said Violet.

Benny said, "Grandfather, I really don't want to pick up glass. I want to see that talking horse."

Mr. Alden thought it over. Then he said, "That's up to you, Benny. You're old enough to take care of yourself. If you'd rather walk two miles and see the horse, go ahead. You heard Al say we could stay here two hours."

Henry said, "I thought you were too sleepy to do anything. You said you didn't sleep at all last night."

"Well, I am sleepy. When I get back to the caboose I'm going to take a nap. Al told me I couldn't miss the path through the woods. I'll go and see the horse first, and then I'll go into the little caboose and go to sleep. And don't any of you open the door. Don't even peek at me and wake me up." He started off.

Grandfather called, "Don't get lost, Benny."

"I'll find my way all right. If I get lost, I can eat nuts and berries. Children always eat nuts and berries when they get lost," Benny said, laughing at his own joke.

"Don't be late, either," Grandfather called again. "The train won't wait for you, you know."

"Yes, I know. I guess I can walk a mile and back in two hours!"

Violet watched Benny as he went into the deep woods. She said to Henry, "I don't like it. You go with him."

Henry said, "No, Violet. I don't think I ought to tell him what to do. Benny must learn to live his own life and make his own mistakes. We all must."

"Good!" said Grandfather. "Benny will never learn if you look after him all the time, Henry."

The Aldens picked up so much glass that they had to get a paper bag from the caboose to put it in. Suddenly a man put his head out of the factory window and called, "Would you like to see the glass factory?"

"We'd like to very much, sir," said Grandfather. They all went up the steps and met the man at the door.

"I'll show you first how we make pressed glass. Just follow me. My name is Lidstone."

"I'm James Alden," said Grandfather, "and these are my grandchildren."

"Yes, I know," Mr. Lidstone said, smiling. "I guess you are the people traveling by caboose. Everyone is talking about it. You young people may know how glass is made," he went on as they went into another room. "We mix sand and potash and get it so hot it melts. Then we pour it and press the glass into molds."

It was exciting to watch the workmen pouring the melted glass into fancy molds.

"Oh, what beautiful colors!" said Violet.

"And so many," said Jessie.

"These small dishes are finished," said Mr. Lidstone. He pointed at a table. "You may choose any color you want. They will be gifts to remember us by."

"Thank you, sir," said Henry. "My young brother Benny isn't here. He went to see the talking horse. Too bad he is missing this."

"Then you choose one for him," said Mr. Lidstone.

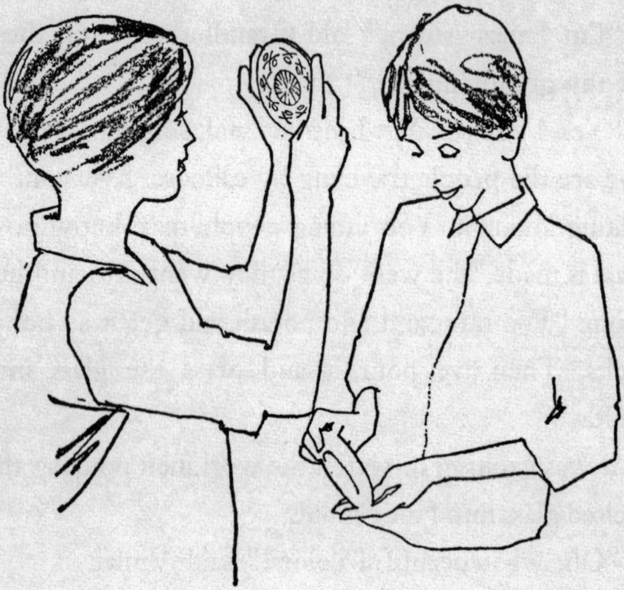

"Benny would choose red, I'm sure of that," said Jessie. She picked up a red dish for Benny.

"Let me tell you something about that color," said Mr. Lidstone. "We use real gold to make red. In the old days, the glassmakers threw in gold dollars to make red. Have you all decided on your colors?"

Jessie held up a blue dish for answer. Violet had a violet one, and Henry chose green. Mr. Alden had a bright yellow one.

"Now come and see the glassblowers," said Mr. Lidstone. He took them to another room. Three men were blowing glass. A worker picked up a lump of melted glass on a pipe and began to blow.

"Oh, that's going to be a pitcher," whispered Jessie.

The big glass ball on the end of the pipe grew larger and larger. Then suddenly it grew smaller. The man jerked off the pipe.

"No, it's a vase," said Violet. "Isn't it wonderful how they do that?"

In another room the Aldens watched a row of men and women making designs on glass dishes. Mr. Lidstone said, "This is very fine work. Each person here is an artist."

The Aldens could have watched them all afternoon, but they knew they had to get back to the train. They thanked Mr. Lidstone for their visit and went back to the caboose with their new dishes.

Jessie said, "Benny will like to know that his red dish was made with gold."

Mr. Alden looked at his watch and frowned. "It's

much later than I thought," he said. "Only five minutes before we go. I hope Benny is in the small caboose taking his nap."

Jessie said, "He's probably been back a long time because we stayed so long in the factory. Remember what he said. He told us not to go into that caboose and wake him up."

"I'd like to peek in and see if he's there," said Violet.

"Don't do it, Violet," said Henry. "He'll come out at supper time. You wait and see."

The train gave two whistles. Then it started. Off went the Aldens. Soon Glass Factory Junction was far behind them.

CHAPTER 6

Benny's Adventure

While the Aldens were at the glass factory, Benny was walking through the woods. The path was very poor. Sometimes he thought that he was not on the path at all—and he was right.

Benny knew that he was supposed to go a mile, but he knew that he had walked much further than that. After a while, he did come to a main road. He looked both ways. At last he saw a house almost hidden by trees. Two boys were playing in the yard.

Benny walked toward the boys and called, "Do you own a talking horse?"

"Yes, we do," said the older boy. "Want to see him?"

Benny nodded. "Yes, that's what I came for," he said.

The boys led Benny to a large shed. The little boy asked, "How did you hear about old Major?"

"Mr. Shaw, the stationmaster at Pinedale, told me," said Benny. "He said Major was a circus horse."

"That's right," said the boy. "Cho-Cho the clown works for Mr. Shaw. He used to own our horse, but he sold him to us."

The three boys stopped at the door of the shed, and sure enough, inside was the horse.

The big boy said, "Well, Major, are you glad to see this stranger?"

The horse tossed his head and looked at Benny. The boys took the horse out of the shed.

"Are you afraid of the stranger?" asked the boy.

Major shook his head from side to side. His beautiful white mane blew in the wind. Benny was delighted.

"Could I ask him a question?"

"Sure," said the boy. "Maybe he will answer you."

"How much are two and one?" asked Benny in a

loud voice. The horse pawed the ground three times.

"Sit down, Major," said the boy. The horse sat down like a dog.

"What do you want to do now?" asked the boy. The horse lay down on his side and shut his eyes.

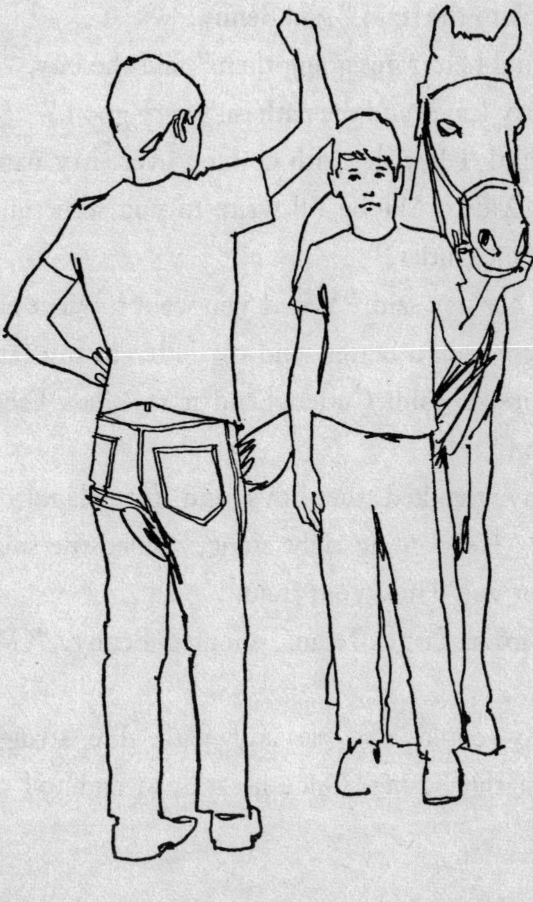

"He's a wonder," said Benny. "I suppose you will never sell him?"

"Well, it's possible," said the boy. "Major is lonesome here. You're the first visitor we have had for two weeks. Where are you going from here?"

"Back to the train," said Benny.

"You'd better get going then," said the boy. "The train may leave, and the path isn't very good."

"I think I lost the path coming over. My name is Benny Alden. Maybe I'll write to you sometime. Is your name Cutler?"

The big boy said, "Yes. If you want to write about the horse, you'd better send the letter to my father. His name is John Cutler. Send it to Glass Factory Junction."

Benny thanked the boys and turned into the woods. "Keep going right along," called the smaller boy, "or you'll miss your train."

"I'll go as fast as I can," shouted Benny. "Goodbye!"

Benny could not see any path. He struggled through the bushes. Once he tripped and fell on a stone and cut his knee. At last he said to himself, "I am certainly lost. But I know I'm going the right way toward the station."

Soon the path was better, and he began to run. In a minute he saw a little house that he had not passed on his way to the Cutlers. On the step sat a little boy and his mother.

"Look, Mom," said the little boy. "Somebody's coming."

Benny was very glad to see some people. He said, "I want to catch that freight train. Do you think I can make it?"

"No," said the woman. "I'm sorry. We just heard one whistle already. When it whistles again, the train will start. You can't go fast enough to catch it."

"I have to go just the same," said Benny. "I lost the path when I came over. It took me a lot longer than I expected."

The boy said, "Did you go to see the talking horse?"

"Yes, I did," said Benny. "He was fun, but now I've lost my family."

The boy looked at his mother. Then he said, "I'll go with you."

"You don't look old enough," said Benny.

"Oh, yes, I am," said the boy. "I know the way to the station anyway, and I know every single train that goes by."

"Yes, he does," said the woman. "In summer he hasn't anything else to do except watch the trains."

"Come on," said the boy. He led the way, running.

Benny followed him as well as he could.

"What's your name?" he called to the boy. "Mine is Benny Alden."

"Charley Jackson," said the boy, running faster. "Be careful! This is a bad place!" It was too late. Benny had tripped over a great bunch of vines and fallen again on his sore knee.

"I'm sorry," said Charley, coming back. "I guess you're not used to running in the deep woods."

"No," said Benny. "But I ought to have seen those vines."

"You're caught for sure," said Charley. "This is what I use for a knife." He took a thin flat stone out of his pocket. He started to cut one vine after another.

"Well, that stone is sharp," said Benny.

"Yes," said Charley. "I have to carry something. I'm always needing a knife in these woods. There you are. Pull your foot out now."

Benny started to get up.

"Look out! Don't touch that!" said Charley. "That's poison ivy!"

"Oh, I see it is now," said Benny. "I wasn't even looking. A good thing you stopped me, because that stuff poisons me."

When Benny was on his feet, the boys ran on.

"Don't feel bad about falling," Charley called back. "I've seen grown-up men fall down in here, going to see the talking horse. I know where you went this morning. You weren't on the path at all. This is bad, but that is worse. Oh, oh! There goes the whistle again."

"And now I've lost my train," said Benny.

Charley slowed down. "What are you going to do?"

"Well," said Benny, "I'll have to go to the railroad station just the same. You see my grandfather and my big brother and two sisters are on that train."

"Won't they make the train wait for you?" asked Charley.

Benny shook his head. "No. I told them that when I came back I would take a nap. I told them not to open the door and wake me up. So they will think I'm sleeping in the caboose."

"Caboose!" said Charley. "I never heard of such a thing—traveling on a caboose!"

The boys walked slowly now.

"Yes," said Benny. "We are taking a trip in two cabooses. I've been trying to think what my grandfather will do when he finds I'm not there. I'm sure he will come back to this station. There's no other place for him to go."

"I guess you're right," said Charley. "That's the only road except this path. This road just goes a long way around by Cutlers."

"My family won't know I am lost until it's supper time," said Benny. "Oh, boy, am I hungry!"

"What did you have for lunch?"

"I didn't have any lunch," said Benny.

"No wonder you're hungry," said Charley. "Do you like apples?"

"I love them!" said Benny. "I could eat about a dozen right now."

The boys reached the station. The door was locked. The factory was shut, too. The train had gone.

"You sit down on the doorstep," said Charley. "I'll be right back."

Off he ran into the woods. In no time he was back again with his pockets full of small red apples.

"Have an apple," he said. "These are wild. Not very good."

"They are delicious!" said Benny. "You eat some, too, Charley."

"I had my lunch," said Charley, "but it's supper time now." He took an apple.

The two boys sat on the steps of the station.

"Charley, did you ever hear of a clown named Cho-Cho and a diamond necklace?" Benny asked.

"Oh, yes. Everybody knows about that," said Charley. "Cho-Cho used to own the talking horse. My father used to tell me all about it, because the police asked him to watch out for a thin man."

Benny nodded. "And your father never found him?"

"No. That was a long time ago. I don't think they'll ever find him."

The two boys went on eating apples. They waited and waited and waited.

CHAPTER 7

A Wild Ride

Henry, Jessie, Violet, and Grandfather sat quietly in the big caboose. Nobody spoke. The train rattled along.

At last Jessie said, "I can't stand this. I'm going to see if Benny is in the little caboose. I hope you don't mind, Grandfather."

Mr. Alden said, "No, Jessie, I don't mind. I think you are right. He ought to wake up anyway. It's time for supper."

Jessie and Violet opened the door of the little caboose. They took one look. They could see all four bunks. They were empty.

"He's not here!" they called.

"Oh, Grandfather, what shall we do?" said Violet.

Mr. Alden said quickly, "Don't worry, Violet. We'll find him. I'm perfectly sure of that."

Henry said, "Now is the time for those air brakes. We can let the trainmen know we are in trouble."

He went to the desk and turned the lever halfway. The train slowed down at once and stopped.

The Aldens jumped off and met Al running down beside the train to meet them.

"Benny is missing!" shouted Grandfather.

"Missing!" called Al. "What happened?"

"I'll tell you later," said Mr. Alden. "I'm sure he is still at Glass Factory Junction. He went to see the talking horse."

"We can't go back, sir," said Al, frowning. "I'm sorry, but those are the rules. It might cause an accident."

Grandfather nodded. "I understand," he said, "but how can we get back to Glass Factory and find him?"

Al said, "I think you'd better go right along to the next station and get off. That will be Woodstock.

You can hire some kind of a car at the station. Maybe you can catch us at Springdale if you find the boy."

"Oh, we'll find him!" said Grandfather. "We'll find him if we have to cut down the whole woods."

"We'll do all we can," said Al. "We'll make a fast run to Woodstock."

Al ran back to the engine. The Aldens piled into the big caboose. Two whistles, and away they went.

Jessie said, "Grandfather, where do you think Benny really is?"

"Well, my dear, Benny has a good head on his shoulders. He will think it out. When he sees that he has missed the train, he will probably stay right there. I am counting on that. What else could he do?"

"He might telephone," said Violet.

"Well, where would he find a telephone?" asked Mr. Alden. "The station is probably closed, and so is the factory. Anyway, we will hurry back to Glass Factory and see if he is there."

The caboose swayed from side to side.

"We're going faster than usual," said Jessie. "The engineer is helping us."

The whole family was ready to jump off as soon as the train stopped at Woodstock. As they hurried toward the head of the train, they saw Mr. Carr talking to a man in an old station wagon.

Mr. Carr called, "Here is a man who will take you back to Glass Factory. I know him, and he's a good driver."

"Do you know the shortest way?" asked Grandfather, as they all got into the car.

"Yes, sir, we'll come out by the factory and go over the track. There's the station and the woods."

"Right!"

Nobody spoke. The old car bumped along. At last it passed the glass factory and bumped over the railroad track.

"Here's the station," Henry called out, as the car came to a quick stop.

Benny and Charley sat on the step, eating apples. Benny looked up.

"There he is!" said Jessie.

"Oh, Benny!" called Violet.

Benny shouted, "There's my grandfather, Charley." He rushed to the car with an apple in each hand. "I knew it, I knew it! I knew you'd find me," he said over and over. "I got lost and Charley was awfully good to me."

Mr. Alden was in a great hurry, but he took time to thank Charley. He said, "Thank you, Charley. I can't talk long now because we want to catch that train at the next station."

"You can't do it, mister," said Charley. "Don't stop at the next station. Go on to Fairfield and catch it there."

"Thank you," called Mr. Alden.

Charley watched the car as it turned around and

went out of sight. Then he went off through the woods. He had had a wonderful time.

"That boy was right," the driver said. "I won't try to catch the train at Springdale, but I'll go right across to Fairfield."

They passed through Springdale, and no Little North Freight was in sight.

The car raced along. The driver was going to Fairfield, just as Charley had told him. The driver soon took a different road. He said, "When I tell you, be ready to get out."

"You bet we will," said Benny.

"Now!" called the driver. He stopped. The Aldens raced to the station and looked down the track.

"Oh, dear!" said Jessie. "There goes the train. We've missed it!" The big caboose was just disappearing around the bend.

"Never mind," said the driver. "Get right back in the car, and I'll race it to Oak Hill."

"Wait!" cried Violet. "The train is backing up! There is Al on the back platform. He sees us."

"And the conductor, too," said Henry. "They are both waving."

Sure enough, the Little North freight was slowly chug-chugging back to the station.

Grandfather paid the driver, and they all waited in a row until the train came to a stop.

Never was a train crew so glad to see passengers. The engineer blew his whistle. The conductor took a deep breath and helped Mr. Alden up the steps. Al looked at Benny and said, "Don't go off again, young man."

"No, I never will," Benny promised.

The Aldens sat down in the big caboose. Jessie washed off Benny's knee and put on a bandage. Then they all looked at each other. "I'm cold," said Grandfather.

"I'm cold, too," said Violet, shivering.

"You all need food," Al said, going up the ladder. "Remember you haven't had supper, and it's eight o'clock."

Jessie said, "I've an idea. Henry, you make some hot cocoa on the stove in the small caboose. Violet and I will use the stove in Number 777. We'll get up a fine supper in no time."

Jessie opened a can of chicken and heated it. Violet used potato flakes to make mashed potatoes. The girls opened a big can of cherries for dessert.

What a dinner the Aldens had! It was almost nine o'clock before they were through eating.

"I can see some of us are almost asleep," said Henry. He winked at Jessie. Benny's eyes were almost shut. The girls went quietly into the other caboose.

Henry began to help Benny get into bed.

"What about the lower bunk, old man?" said Henry. "Just for one night?"

"OK," said Benny. That was all he could say. He was fast asleep.

CHAPTER 8

The Rainy Day

That night, the Aldens slept and slept. Henry was the first one to wake up. He was in the upper bunk. This was really the lookout with windows on all sides.

"Raining!" said Henry to himself. "Just look at the rain! I think the rain woke me up."

The water was running down all the windows, making a loud tapping sound on the top of the caboose. Henry climbed down and found Mr. Alden and Benny awake.

"It's pouring," said Benny. "I don't like that. I never thought of rain. We can't sit out on the back platform at all."

"Don't worry about that," said Henry. "We'll find plenty to do." He could see the girls walking around in the other caboose.

As Benny dressed, he looked around the big caboose. He thought about Cho-Cho, and Chi-Chi's necklace, and the talking horse.

When the family sat down to breakfast, Mr. Alden said, "Now Ben, tell us how you got lost."

Benny told the whole story. At the end he said, "Grandfather, you can see that Charley needs a knife if he has to use a sharp stone. Do you suppose you and I could give him one?"

"Maybe we could," said Mr. Alden with a smile.

All this time Henry was thinking. He said, "Everything would be all fixed up if we could only find that diamond necklace. Cho-Cho could sell it and buy his horse back. Then maybe the Thin Man would not be afraid to see his friends."

Violet said, "I worry about that Thin Man. And I don't know a thing we can do." She looked out of the window. "Just listen to that rain," she went on. "And look at the trees. They are all bent over in the wind. I never saw it rain so hard. What a storm!"

"I'm sorry," said Jessie, looking out of the window. "I'll tell you why I'm sorry. I didn't plan very well for rain. Today I was going to make a big stew, but I didn't get the meat."

"Never mind, Jessie," said Henry. "I have a raincoat. I'll get off at the next stop and buy whatever you want."

Mr. Alden said, "Mr. Carr told me that we don't make many stops, but the next one is quite a large town. Henry would have time to get meat, because we stay there for half an hour."

"That will be fine," said Jessie. "It will give the stew three hours to cook."

"Make a list of what you need, Jessie," said Henry. "I'll get on my rain things."

Benny said, "Here's an old pair of boots under the sink."

Henry put on his raincoat and pulled a black rain hat over his ears. He pulled on the big boots.

Jessie said, "Here's the list. I hope you can get everything."

Henry was a funny looking sight. He had a red scarf around his neck to hold up his collar. The boots were too big for him. Soon the train went past a big station and stopped above it. Henry opened the door and ran down the steps in the rain. Just as Henry reached the platform, Al met him. The two went off together.

"Good!" said Grandfather. "Al will know where the stores are."

Jessie and Violet began to heat water for dishes. The sink was so small that they washed a few and put them away. Then they washed some more.

"You make your bed now, Benny," said Jessie. "That will give you something to do. And the caboose will look better."

"I'll make all the beds in this Number 777," said Benny. "The top bunk in the lookout is really mine, and I'll sleep there tonight."

The girls peeled onions and potatoes for the stew. They went into the small caboose and made their own beds.

"Ha!" called Benny from the lookout.

"What's the matter?" asked Grandfather.

"Nothing—just the stuffing is coming out of my mattress. It makes me sneeze."

"Yes," said Grandfather, "I've heard you sneeze. I thought you had a cold."

"No," said Benny. "No cold—just stuffing. Some day will you mend my mattress, Jessie?"

"Of course," said Jessie, "but not right now."

Soon Grandfather said, "Here's Henry back again. See him run! He can hardly stand up."

Henry pushed the door open and came in, dripping water all over the floor. "It's a cloud-burst!" he said.

Henry took off his wet things and hung them around the little caboose to dry. Jessie took out the carrots, the beef, milk, and other things that Henry had bought. She filled the biggest kettle with water. In went the onions, the meat, and some salt. She put on the cover.

"Thank you for the newspaper, Henry," said Grandfather. "Rain all day," he went on. "That's what the paper says."

"I don't care," Benny said. "I like it."

"I thought you didn't like it," said Henry laughing.

Benny said, "I've been thinking about Number 777. I'm sure it does have a mystery. And a rainy day is a good one to work on a mystery. You know that necklace may be right in plain sight."

"It couldn't be," Henry said. "We'd have seen it, Benny."

"I mean it could be *in* something we look at everyday," said Benny.

"Now that's a good idea." Henry looked at his brother. "I believe you might be right, Ben," he said. "I don't think the police looked in everything after the Thin Man ran away. I'm sure they thought he stole it."

"Let's begin again and look everything over," Benny said.

They began by the door. Henry took the old stove apart. Jessie laughed and took the lamp apart. Violet began to take the canned vegetables off the shelves, to look under the papers.

Benny went to the bookcase beside the desk. He

shook every book. A few old papers fell out. Benny looked at every one, but he could not find a single clue. He began to put the books back. Some of them were quite tall.

As Benny started to put the books on the shelf, he saw something he had not seen before. It was an old postcard tacked up on the wall behind the books. Benny took out the thumbtack and looked at the postcard. His heart beat faster when he saw that it was addressed to Cho-Cho. He turned it over and read the three lines written there.

"Look!" he shouted. "Look at this, Grandfather!" He was so excited that he dropped the card. He picked it up and watched his grandfather as he read,

"If you are a Clown,
Be on the lookout
For things in a crown."

"Well, well," said Mr. Alden. "This is a real clue, Benny! It is signed right here by Chi-Chi."

Jessie said, "Surely things in a crown would be diamonds!"

"I do think you're right," said Henry. "But it still doesn't mean much to me."

"It didn't mean much to Cho-Cho," agreed Mr. Alden, "or he would have told us about it. Or maybe he never found it."

"He must have," said Benny. "It went through the postoffice. It's a clue all right. Perhaps there was something in the shape of a crown where she hid the necklace. We'll have to think about it."

Jessie jumped up. "I'll have to think about the stew! Just smell it!"

She cut up the potatoes and carrots and put them into the stew. When they were done, Violet got five dishes out of the closet. Some were bowls and some were soup plates.

Jessie served the stew. She said, "We have rolls and milk and the stew, and that's all."

"That's enough," said Grandfather. "This is delicious, Jessie."

The rain poured down all day. Mr. Alden said, "This is almost a hurricane. I hope tomorrow will be pleasant."

Mr. Alden got his wish. When the Aldens woke up the next morning, the sun was shining.

About the middle of the morning, there was a loud knock on the door of the caboose.

CHAPTER 9

Engineer Benny

The knocking on the caboose door grew louder and louder.

"Who can that be?" Henry asked as he went to open the door. "Oh, it's Al! Come right in!"

Al said, "I came to invite you to dinner at noon in our work-caboose."

"What fun!" said Benny. "Are you going to do the cooking?"

"Yes," said Al. "I'm the cook. But this is a surprise. We'll unlock the door, and you can walk into our caboose at noon."

"Could I ever see the engine?" asked Benny.

"I'll ask Mr. Davis," said Al. "He's the engineer. I think he may let you run the engine. He'll show you the dead-man's pedal, anyway."

"What's the dead-man's pedal?" asked Benny.

"A secret," said Al. "See you at noon."

At noon the family walked into the work-caboose. Mr. Carr was there, waiting. He said, "Mr. Davis is stopping the train. He says Benny can walk down to the engine."

Benny said, "I suppose I couldn't walk down on top of the train?"

"No," said Mr. Carr laughing, "you could not."

When the train stopped, Al and Mr. Carr and Benny walked down to the engine. When they were safely aboard, the train started again.

"Now you sit down in the engineer's seat, Benny," said Mr. Davis. "Here is the dead-man's pedal. I keep my foot on that pedal all the time. If anything happened to me, my foot would slip off, and the train would stop. The air brakes would stop the train."

"What *could* happen to you?" Benny asked.

"Well, I might have a heart attack."

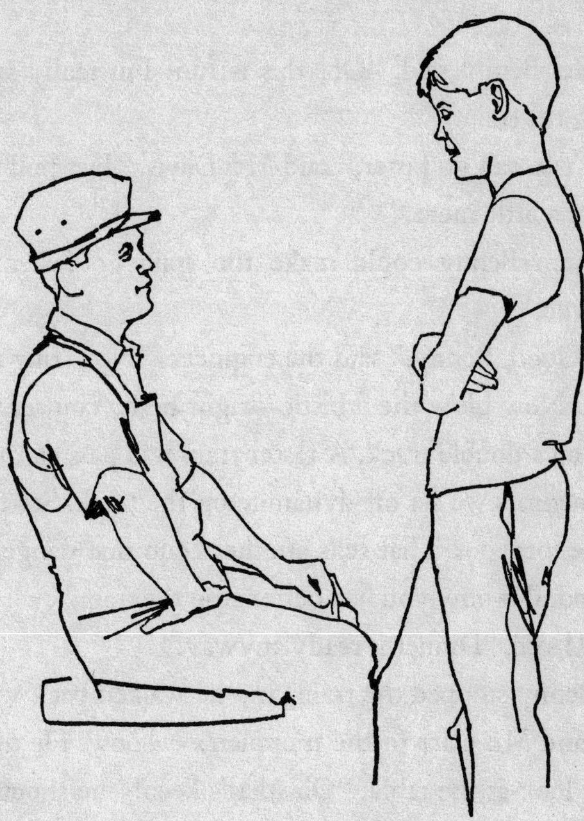

"Oh, I hope you won't," said Benny.

Mr. Davis laughed. "No, I don't expect to, but that pedal is a nice thing to have. Now, Benny, pull this lever and the train will start."

Benny pulled the lever. The big engine began to

move. Benny said, "Oh, this is fun! I'm really running the train."

"You can go faster," said Mr. Davis. "Just pull the lever a little more."

Soon Benny could make the train go faster or slower.

"Good, Benny," said the engineer. "Now ring the bell. Now blow the whistle—right here. You see we are on a double track. A faster train will pass us later. Sometimes we set off dynamite on the track. See this little torpedo? That tells another train that danger is ahead. But now you had better stop the train."

Al said, "Dinner is ready anyway."

Benny stopped the train, and he walked back with Al and Mr. Carr to the trainmen's caboose. He took one look at the table. "Oh, that's keen!" he shouted. "Everyone has a talking horse!"

On each plate was an animal made of a big frankfurter. The legs were four smaller sausages. The heads were pickles. The tails were carrot curls.

Al said, "We have plenty of extra frankfurters, so eat all you want."

They all sat down at the table. Mr. Davis started up the engine again.

"This is the first party we ever had on this caboose," Mr. Carr said.

"I never thought I'd ever be eating dinner in a caboose with a train crew. Can I run the Diesel again after dinner?" asked Benny.

"Sure," said Mr. Carr. "Mr. Davis says he likes to have help. It gives him a rest."

Grandfather laughed.

After dinner, Mr. Davis stopped the train again, and Benny walked back to the engine. Mr. Davis gave him the engineer's seat, and he pulled the lever. Benny was quite used to it now. He kept his eyes on the two tracks ahead, but there was not much to see.

Mr. Davis said, "Very soon that fast train will pass right by us on that other track. Just slow down while it goes by."

"My, this is a lonesome place," said Benny. "No houses."

"No," said Mr. Davis, "there isn't a house for miles."

"A few trees," said Benny, "two railroad tracks, and us. And that's all."

Suddenly Benny saw something on the track ahead.

"Oh, look, Mr. Davis!" he shouted. "What's that?"

Mr. Davis had seen the same thing. He grabbed the lever. "Let me do it, boy!"

He stopped the train as quickly as he could. It was not a minute too soon.

"Well, that was good luck," he said. A narrow escape!"

Al was on top of the train. He took one look at the tracks ahead. Then he climbed quickly down the ladder and ran back toward the end of the train.

"Why is Al running?" Benny asked. "I can't see anything back there."

"The fast train on the other track is due any minute," Mr. Davis said. "They won't see the trouble in time to stop. We have to warn them."

"How?" asked Benny. "What can we do in time to stop them?"

"Al is going to put a torpedo on that other track behind us. When that fast freight runs over the torpedo, the engineer will stop his train."

"What is that thing on the tracks ahead of us?" Benny asked.

"A tree. Let's get out and see it. You see it has fallen right across both tracks."

By now the rest of the Aldens knew that something was wrong. They had seen Al running past them, and they knew that the train had stopped very suddenly. Violet asked, "Oh, do you suppose anything has happened to Benny?"

"Let's go and see," said Grandfather. When the family reached the front of the engine, they could see Benny standing beside the men. Mr. Davis and Mr. Carr each had a shovel and an axe.

It was a sight to see. An enormous tree had fallen across both tracks. Wet earth was piled high on one side. It had come from a high bank above the track.

"The storm did this," said Mr. Davis.

The two men began to chop off branches. The Aldens pulled the branches away without a word.

They threw them down the bank out of the way. Everyone worked fast. Al shoveled the earth off the track.

Mr. Davis and Mr. Carr were listening for something. The engineer took out his watch and looked at it. "That train ought to be along any minute," he said.

Suddenly there was a great BANG! Everyone jumped. Violet covered her ears. "What an awful noise!" she said.

"That's the torpedo!" said Benny. He looked down the track and saw the other train. It had stopped. Men were running toward them.

One man shouted, "The storm did this, I suppose?"

"Right!" said Mr. Carr. "The wind blew the tree down, and the rain washed down all this earth. It's a wonder it didn't wash out the track under us."

The new train crew had shovels and axes, too. They went right to work. Soon both tracks were clear, and the fast train could go along. The Aldens waved and watched it out of sight.

Benny said, "I guess you'd better run the engine, Mr. Davis. It's too exciting for me."

The Aldens thanked the men for the fine dinner. Then they started back to their own caboose. As they walked along, Jessie said, "I've had enough excitement for one day. Let's do something quiet."

"You might mend my mattress, Jessie. That will be quiet enough," said Benny.

"Good!" agreed Jessie. "Just the thing. I will mend your mattress right now."

The minute the train started, Jessie got a big needle and heavy thread from Violet's workbag. She sat down at the big table.

"This is just what I meant," she said. "A quiet change for everybody."

CHAPTER 10

Curing Sneezes

It was quiet in the caboose while Jessie laid out Violet's scissors and threaded a needle. Grandfather sat by his window as he always did, but the others sat around the table with Jessie.

Benny asked, "Are you going to mend my mattress way up in the lookout?"

Jessie laughed. "No, I couldn't work up there. I think we shall have to take it down."

"I'll do it," said Henry. "Come on, Ben, give me a hand."

The boys pulled at the mattress. It was heavy and hard to hold. But at last the long mattress slid down from the lookout. The boys laid it on the table.

Jessie sat down right in front of the hole. She looked at the mattress. It was covered with old black leather.

"I wonder if this is the same mattress the circus people used," she said. "It looks old enough."

"Remember I told you," said Grandfather, "that my friend said we could have new covers if we wanted them."

"I remember," said Jessie. "But we're glad we took the caboose just as it was. No new things." She took a stick and poked at the stuffing. She said, "A lot of stuffing is coming out. I think I'll pull out a little more. That will make it more even."

She did so. Out came a big bunch of stuffing. She picked it to pieces because it was rather hard. Then she pushed it back with the long stick. Then she began to sew. Everybody watched.

"That's like a baseball," said Benny.

"Yes, it's called baseball stitch," said Jessie. "The needle goes in one side and then in the other."

When it was done, Benny said, "That's fine, Jessie. Would you want to mend the other side, too?"

"Of course! I might as well do it all."

Jessie went around and sat down on the other side of the mattress. She said, "This side isn't as bad."

"I'll help you pull out the stuffing," said Benny. "I'm used to it. Every night I sneeze and sneeze."

He pulled out a lot of stuffing with the stick. "Let's take it all out, Jessie," he said. "Then it really will be smooth. It's so lumpy." He dug out some more.

Henry laughed. He said, "You have lots of troubles, Ben. Lumps and sneezes. Why didn't you say so?"

"I did say so. I asked Jessie a long time ago to mend my mattress, didn't I? What's all this?"

"Well, what is it?" asked Henry.

Benny began saying "Hey! Hey! Hey!" He pulled at the stuffing, and out dropped a little package done up in paper!

"Oh, *Benny*!" said Jessie.

Benny's hands shook as he tried to untie the string.

"Oh, shucks!" he said. "I can't untie that string. I'll tear it open."

He tore the paper and shook it. A long chain fell out that sparkled with every color of the rainbow. Benny picked up the chain and hung it on one finger. The light made it shine with blue and yellow and green and flashing red. Everyone said, "O-ooo!"

"Benny!" called Mr. Alden in a loud voice from his chair. "Let me see that!"

Benny gave the shining string to his grandfather.

"Children!" said Grandfather. "This is that diamond necklace! Real diamonds, I'm sure."

"That big one in the middle is just the color of my red dish," said Benny.

"I'm sure that is a ruby. If it is a real ruby, it is worth more than the diamonds." Grandfather gazed at it.

Henry said, "This is wonderful! Think what it means! This certainly belongs to Cho-Cho. He can sell it for hundreds of dollars."

"And get back his talking horse," said Benny.

The Aldens passed the necklace from hand to hand. They all watched it sparkle in the light. Violet said, "I can see a beautiful violet color as I turn it."

"And I can see red," said Benny, twisting it.

"I'll tell you what we can do," said Grandfather. "Al says the next stop is a big city. It will surely have a good jewelry store. We can take the necklace there and ask them how much it is worth. They will know if the diamonds are real."

Jessie added, "Then we'll have something to tell Cho-Cho."

Violet said slowly, "I was thinking of the Thin Man. He didn't hide it here, did he, Grandfather?"

"No, certainly not. I'm sure this was Chi-Chi's own hiding place. Probably nobody slept in this lookout for years. I'm sure the owner's wife would not take the upper bunk. She'd sleep in the lower one."

"Just let me see that necklace again," said Jessie. "Isn't it beautiful!" They passed the necklace around again.

Henry gave the necklace back to Benny. He said, "How in the world did Chi-Chi expect her husband to find it?"

"Maybe she didn't want Cho-Cho to find it," said Jessie. "But I can't think why."

Benny was staring at nothing. "Listen!" he shouted. "She *did* want Cho-Cho to find it! Think of that postcard we found behind the books. It said '*Be* on the lookout'—and the necklace was up in the lookout!"

"Benny, I do believe you are right," exclaimed Mr. Alden. "Cho-Cho read that verse, but he didn't understand what his wife meant."

Henry said, "We didn't understand, either, at first." He smiled at Benny.

Jessie settled back. She said, "Now I can hardly wait to get to that big city to see how much the necklace is worth. I was sorry before, because the city means the end of the trip."

Benny shook his head. He said, "No, Jessie, our trip is just half over. We still have the trip back home. And don't forget we still have a mystery. Why did the Thin Man run away? And how can we get word to him that we have found the necklace?"

Henry nodded at his brother. "Good for you, Ben. That is a real question. If the police couldn't find the Thin Man, how can we?"

At last, Jessie picked up her needle. "I'll have to sew up this mattress or Benny won't have any bed to sleep in." She stuffed it carefully and sewed up the corner.

"We'll put it back, Jessie," said Henry. Benny took hold of one end. As he climbed up, Benny began to laugh. He called down,

"If you are a Clown,
Be on the lookout
For things in a crown."

"I'd like to see Cho-Cho's face when he sees the necklace," said Jessie.

"And Mr. Shaw's face, and the Thin Man's face," said Benny.

"If we find him," said Violet.

After the sheets were on the bed again, the family sat down. Henry laughed. He said, "Well, Jessie, I hope this isn't your idea of a quiet, peaceful change!"

"Well, no," said Jessie. "But it certainly was a change!"

CHAPTER 11

Is It Real?

Mr. Alden kept the necklace in his pocket. Next morning, after the housework was done, the train began to slow down. It went clacking onto a siding and came to a stop. The Aldens went down the steps, and there was Al.

Al called to them, "You have two hours here, Mr. Alden. We have to turn the train around. This is the end of the run. Be ready to go back in two hours."

Mr. Alden asked, "Do you know of a good jewelry store?"

"Yes, right over there on Main Street," said Al. "We pass it when we eat lunch at the Golden Horn. Maybe you'd like to eat lunch there, too."

Mr. Alden said, "Come nearer, Al. Look at this." Mr. Alden held up the sparkling necklace.

"Chi-Chi's diamonds!" said Al. "Where in the world did you find them?"

"In my mattress," said Benny. "Jessie was mending it, and there they were."

"I'll tell the crew," said Al. "Oh, will they ever be surprised! I'll tell them this minute. I have to go now anyway."

He rushed off. The Aldens went along Main Street. "What an adventure! It seems strange to see sidewalks and stores again," said Benny.

Jessie said, "Isn't that the Golden Horn way up the street?"

"Yes," said Henry. "I can see it. And the jewelry store is on this side."

Mr. Alden looked at the sign. "Oh, I know all about that store," he said. "It is famous. We can trust them to tell us the truth."

In a few minutes the Aldens went into the store. Mr. Alden went over to a gray-haired man behind a counter.

"How do you do. My name is James Alden. My grandchildren have found a lost article. We know who lost it, but we would like to know how much it is worth."

The gentleman smiled. He expected to see a ring or a pin. He took one glance at the necklace and then looked up. "Well, sir!" he said. "Do you know what you have here?"

"Well, I have some idea," said Mr. Alden, smiling.

The man called to another man, "Come here a minute."

When Mr. Alden put the necklace on the black velvet tray, the second man whistled. He sat down and began to look at the diamonds through a magnifying glass. It took a long time.

Jessie thought, "Will he never tell us?"

At last he took the glass from his eye and said, "Mr. Alden, every stone is a real diamond, and every one is perfect. But the ruby is the best of all. It is a very fine one."

"How much is the necklace worth?" asked Grandfather.

"I wouldn't want to say," said the man. "I would need more time."

Benny spoke up. "Well, could a single man buy a horse and support himself and the horse for a year?"

The man laughed. "Yes, I think so."

"That's just what I wanted to know," said Grandfather. He put the necklace back in his pocket. Then he said, "And now we'd like to buy a knife."

"A knife!" exclaimed the man. He thought that Mr. Alden must want to buy a knife for himself. He took out some beautiful silver pocketknives.

"Oh, no," said Mr. Alden. "I should have told you. We want to buy a knife for a nine-year-old boy. But it must be a strong knife that will fit a boy fourteen years old. Right, Benny?"

"Yes," said Benny. "This boy lives in the woods, and he cuts vines and everything."

The jeweler smiled. "Right over here," he said. "These are all boys' knives. Here is one with all sorts of things in it. Two blades, and a screwdriver—"

"A can opener," said Benny, "and a leather punch. It couldn't be better, Grandfather! Charley will certainly like that one. I can hardly wait to see his face when he opens it."

Mr. Alden paid the man and gave him a card. The man looked at it and said, "Don't I know you? I know the James Alden Library and the James Alden Museum. Are you that James Alden?"

"Well, I suppose I am. We all thank you very much."

When the Aldens were outside, Henry said, "He was surprised about the knife. First a diamond necklace and then a boy's jackknife!"

"Oh, I'm hungry," said Benny, "and here's the Golden Horn."

The other Aldens didn't laugh this time, for they were hungry, too. They all went into the restaurant.

"I'm going to have a pizza," said Jessie.

"So am I," agreed Violet. "We haven't had a pizza for weeks and weeks."

Everyone wanted a pizza. Soon the pies came, hot and bubbling. The tomato sauce was thick with cheese. When lunch was over, Henry said, "We'd better go back to the caboose now."

When they reached the caboose, the whole train had been turned around. They climbed the steps of Number 777.

This time Al walked down on the top of the cars to see if Benny was aboard.

"It's all right, Al," called Benny. "I'm here this time. I try not to make the same mistake twice."

"That's a fine idea," said Al. "It won't take as long to get home as the trip out. It never does. We have more empty boxcars and not so much freight. But we do have to stop at Glass Factory Junction and Pinedale. You can see your friends then. Are you all ready, Mr. Alden?"

Mr. Alden laughed. "Yes, we are ready. We have many things to do before we stop anywhere."

"I can believe that. You folks would always think up something to do. That's sure. So here we go!"

In a minute the train began to move slowly toward home.

CHAPTER 12

Mysterious Message

The train was creeping along. It had hardly left the freight yard in the city.

"I wonder why we don't go faster," said Henry. He looked out of the window.

Jessie said, "Maybe they have to go slowly when they have just turned the train around."

But then the train stopped.

"Now what's the matter?" asked Benny. "I'm sure Al will tell us if there is anything wrong."

"Mr. Carr will tell us," said Grandfather.

As he spoke, Mr. Carr came down the ladder and tapped on the door. Henry opened it.

"Don't be worried," said Mr. Carr. "We are having a little trouble with the engine. The men are starting to fix it already. You'll just have to sit here for a bit."

"What is wrong?" asked Grandfather.

"The waterline broke, but Mr. Davis says we'll be off in an hour."

"An hour!" said Benny. "I thought nothing could happen to a Diesel."

"Well, young man, plenty can happen. We never know. I'm sure you folks can think of things to do." He laughed. "You can't help us this time, so just amuse yourselves." He walked quickly away.

The Aldens sat down in Number 777 and looked at each other.

"I don't mind waiting an hour," said Jessie.

Henry said, "If we really can't help the men, we can think about the Thin Man. We ought to let him know we found the diamonds."

"How can we let him know if we can't find him?" asked Violet.

"There must be some way," said Benny. "That

poor man wasn't to blame at all. Just think how he must feel."

Jessie said, "I've always been sorry for him. Of course he made a mistake to run away. That's the worst thing he could have done."

Benny nodded. "He made a mistake all right. But the police were so sure he stole the necklace, I don't blame him, really."

"You don't blame him, Ben?" asked Grandfather, looking right at his grandson.

"No, I don't. *We* wouldn't want to be arrested, would we? Even if we hadn't done anything wrong?"

Violet said, "I wouldn't, I'm sure. I wonder where he went. And how could he earn a living? Somebody would be sure to see him."

"It's a mystery still," said Jessie. "It happened so long ago. The Thin Man could be anywhere."

"He must be somewhere," said Benny. "And that's what I'm going to do. I'm going to think of some way to send him a message. He ought to be told."

Henry winked. "We might get an airplane to do skywriting."

Benny stood up. "Boy, that gives me an idea!" he said. "What about radio? We could get a radio station to send a message."

Henry nodded.

Jessie asked, "Henry, what would you say on a radio? We can't say diamonds or necklace because everyone will answer."

"I'd say a lost article," said Henry. "And tell him to come to Pinedale. That will give him time to get there."

Benny sat down at the desk. "Let's write this down," he said. "Then it will be ready when we need it. We'll begin, 'Notice to Thin Man.' OK, Henry?"

"That's fine," said Henry. "There aren't many men who are called thin men."

In a few minutes Benny had written this piece. He read it aloud to his family.

> Notice to Thin Man:
> Chi-Chi's lost article has been found.
> She hid it herself. Please come Thursday
> to Pinedale and Number 777.

"Good!" said Henry. "I should think he could understand that, wherever he is. And now where will we find a radio station?"

"I know!" shouted Benny. "Right here in this big city. Will you help us, Grandfather?"

"Certainly," said Mr. Alden, getting up. "We'll have time if we get a taxi and hurry."

"I'm ready," said Benny.

"You and Ben go, Grandfather," said Henry. "Two can hurry faster than five. We'll walk down to the engine and tell Mr. Carr where you are."

Mr. Alden and Benny got off the caboose and walked quickly back to Main Street.

"A taxi driver will know where the radio station is," said Mr. Alden. "Let's ask this one."

In ten minutes Benny and his grandfather were standing in the radio office. Grandfather quickly told the man what he wanted. When the man read the notice, he smiled.

"You sit down right here," he said, "and you'll hear what I say. This station reaches for miles and miles."

Benny said, "Will you keep on saying it? He may not be near a radio."

"I will, young man."

"My grandfather will let you know when we have an answer," said Benny.

"You seem sure that this man will answer," said the radio man.

"Oh, yes, I am," said Benny. "He'll be so pleased."

After Mr. Alden had thanked the man, he told Benny to wait. "I have to make a few telephone calls," he said.

Benny was used to this. Grandfather was always telephoning.

When the taxi returned to the train, the men were still working on the waterline. Mr. Carr called, "Ten minutes more will do it!"

"Good!" Mr. Alden called back.

When the family sat down again in the caboose, Mr. Alden said, "Let me see. We spent five days on the train coming out. We should get to Pinedale the day after tomorrow."

Benny said, "That will give the Thin Man nearly

two days to get to Pinedale. Oh, I hope he listens to the radio!"

Jessie had a surprise for them. "See what Mr. Carr gave me. A transistor radio." She took a tiny radio out of her bag and set it on the table.

"Good for Mr. Carr," said Grandfather. "Just what we need."

Almost at once a voice gave the notice. They could hear every word.

"The same man!" said Benny.

Then the train started. Soon they were rolling along to make up time.

Jessie said, "Let's not forget Charley. We see him first at Glass Factory before we ever get to Pinedale."

"And how will we ever find Charley?" asked Benny. "It seems as if we are always looking for lost people or lost things. You won't want to walk through the woods, Grandfather, as I did."

"I certainly don't expect to walk through any woods," said Mr. Alden. "But we'll find him."

Everyone helped Jessie with the cooking. They swept out both cabooses and made everything neat.

They stopped once for milk. They had to wear sweaters this time when they sat on the back platform. The leaves were starting to turn red and yellow, and the country was beautiful. All the time they talked about their friends in Glass Factory Junction and Pinedale. The train rattled along faster and faster.

After a day and a half, Benny said, "That didn't really seem long. And we are almost at Glass Factory. Let's see if Charley is there."

The Aldens didn't need to worry. Charley was standing on the platform when Number 777 came to a stop. The two Cutler boys were there with their father. Mr. Lidstone from the factory was there. The Aldens jumped down.

"How did you know we were coming today?" asked Benny.

Mr. Lidstone laughed and said, "This is the only time for Number 777 to come through here, and you'd have to be on it. And we had some good reasons to expect you."

Benny ran right over to Charley. "Something for you, Charley," he said. "You were so good to me when I was lost." He gave him the knife. Charley was very much pleased. But when he opened it, he was more pleased than ever.

"Oh, a screwdriver," he said. "And I've always needed something to punch holes with. This knife will do everything! And how is your knee?"

"Fine," said Benny. "And thanks to you, I didn't get poison ivy!"

Mr. Alden was walking over to Mr. Cutler who owned the talking horse. They began to speak in low voices. All at once they all heard a strange sound behind the station.

"That sounds like a horse!" shouted Benny.

"It is a horse," said the Cutler boy. "The talking horse. Didn't you know?"

"No," said Henry. "That's just like Grandfather."

"He telephoned to us," said the boy, laughing.

"Yes, Major's going on the same train with you, in a boxcar," added Mr. Cutler.

Everyone rushed around to see the horse. There stood Major, pawing the ground and shaking his head. He was tied to a tree. Mr. Cutler untied the rope and led him to the train. A boxcar was ready. A heavy board led up into the boxcar. Mr. Cutler went up the board first, and Major followed him.

When Major was safely in his boxcar, the whistle blew and the train started. Everyone waved to the Aldens.

Charley said, "I don't think I'll ever see Benny Alden again."

"Well," said the Cutler boy, "you've got a knife to remember him by."

Charley thought for a minute.

Then he said, "But I don't need a knife to remind me of Benny Alden. Nobody could ever forget Benny."

CHAPTER 13

Surprise for Cho-Cho

It was not far from Glass Factory to Pinedale. Suddenly Jessie said, "Grandfather, let's have a party for the train crew and the people at Pinedale. We have big boxes of cookies. And I could use up all the canned orange juice and mix it with coke. Do you think it would be good?"

"We can try it and see," said Henry.

Jessie put one bottle of coke into a big pitcher. Then she put in a cup of orange juice.

"Not bad!" Henry said.

Violet tried it. She said, "It really is good."

The train rattled along. Soon they heard the whistle up in the engine.

Mr. Alden said, "Remember Cho-Cho doesn't know we have found the necklace. And he doesn't know that his horse is on the train."

"Do you think he'll be at the station?" asked Henry.

"Yes, I do. Mr. Shaw has to be at the station, and Cho-Cho helps him."

When the train stopped, all the Aldens looked out.

Benny said, "The very same men! Six of them."

The Aldens hurried down the steps. Everyone began to shake hands.

Grandfather said to Benny, "You found the necklace. You give it to Cho-Cho."

Benny couldn't wait a second. He shouted, "Cho-Cho! Come here a minute! See what we found. We found it in the mattress in the lookout!"

Cho-Cho took the paper package. He did not understand what Benny was talking about. "Open it!" said Benny. "It's yours!"

Everyone was watching. Cho-Cho took off the paper, and there hung the diamond necklace shining in the sun.

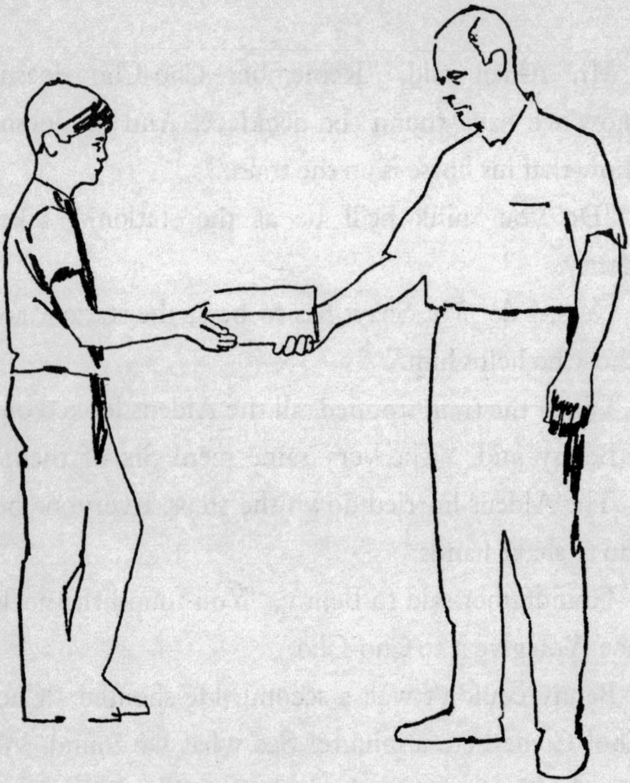

Cho-Cho began to shake. He said, "Chi-Chi! Your necklace!"

"Look out. He's going to faint," said Mr. Shaw.

"Oh, no, I'm not," said Cho-Cho. "I'm going right to Glass Factory and buy my horse back. Mr. Cutler will sell him when I show him these diamonds."

"I'm sure he will," said Mr. Alden, smiling.

"We'll go with you, Cho-Cho," said Benny. "Come on, we'll get on the train."

"No, boy," said Cho-Cho. "That train is going the other way."

His voice was quite loud. Major heard his master, and he did his best to answer with a loud whinny.

"Major!" shouted Cho-Cho. He could not hurry fast enough.

Al and Henry had the board ready. And off walked Major without a single slip. He stopped beside his master.

Cho-Cho put his arms around the horse's neck and began to talk to him.

"Oh, Major, I was so lonesome for you!"

Then nobody could believe it. The answer came back, "I was lonesome for you, too."

"That sounded just like a horse," shouted Benny.

Mr. Carr laughed. "What does a horse sound like, Benny?" he asked.

"The horse didn't really talk though, did he?" asked Benny.

"Well, no, I can't really talk," came the horse's voice.

Everyone looked at Cho-Cho, but nobody could see his lips move. The horse said, "My master is a clever man, as you say. I have missed him very much."

Mr. Davis said, "People would pay money to hear Cho-Cho and his horse talking together."

"I would myself," said Mr. Alden.

"I'm hungry, Cho-Cho," said Major. Still Cho-Cho did not move his lips.

Benny was glad to hear that. "We're all hungry, Major. We are going to have a party right now."

Henry said, "Everyone come into the caboose and help bring the things down."

Mr. Carr came down with a big plate of cookies. Mr. Davis had another. Henry and Al came down with the new drink in big pitchers.

"This is our Alden orange-coke special," said Henry.

All the people stood around eating. Mr. Alden said to Cho-Cho, "Do you want to sell the necklace?"

"Yes," said Cho-Cho. "Diamonds are no good to me."

"Do you know what you want to do with the money?" asked Mr. Alden.

"Oh, yes, I thought of that long ago. I can buy a truck with a horse-trailer on the back. This would be a little home for Major and a home for me. I've always wanted to travel around and show my talking horse."

"Good!" said Mr. Alden. "I wish I could go with you. I am going to New York soon anyway. I shall be glad to sell the necklace for you."

Cho-Cho gave the necklace to Mr. Alden. He said, "I'm afraid I couldn't do it myself. But I could get the trailer."

"Could you?" asked Grandfather in surprise.

"Yes, I could," said Cho-Cho. "It's not far. I think Mr. Shaw will take me tomorrow in his car."

"Tomorrow? Tonight!" said Mr. Shaw. "Why wait till tomorrow, Cho-Cho?"

Suddenly Mr. Davis said, "Listen! Here comes a motorcycle. I wonder who that is."

A large man dashed up on a motorcycle. He got off quickly and went right over to Cho-Cho.

"Don't you know me?" he asked.

Cho-Cho looked him over. "No. I never saw you before in my life," he said.

"You've seen me hundreds of times," said the man.

"*I've* seen you," shouted Benny. "You're a special postman, and your name is Sid Weston."

The postman shook his head. "No, my name is not Sid Weston any more. My name is John Mann. I'm the Thin Man!"

Cho-Cho looked at him more closely. "You *are* the Thin Man, John!" he exclaimed. "But you aren't thin any more."

"I hope not," said the Thin Man. "I worked hard enough to gain all this weight. It took me over a year. But it was worth it. Nobody ever knew me."

Cho-Cho said slowly, "John, tell me why did you ever run away if you didn't take those diamonds?"

"I want to tell you," said the Thin Man. "Nobody believed what I said, and I had a lot of money on me. I didn't have a chance to hide it. I had been saving all my money for a long time. I didn't want to stay in the circus all my life. The money was sewed in the lining of my coat."

Henry nodded. "That would mean trouble for you. If the police had found all that money, they would think you had stolen the diamonds for sure."

"And sold them," said Benny.

"Right," said the Thin Man. "You're a smart boy. I went to a lonely place and lived in a tumble-down house, and nobody found out where I went."

Mr. Shaw said, "You must have been eating all the time."

"Yes, that's all I did," said the Thin Man. "I would walk to a big city and get all the food I could carry. Then I just sat around and ate."

"I never heard of such a thing," said Mr. Alden. "I suppose when you were fat enough, you looked for a job as a postman."

"Yes, I used to be a postman before I joined the circus. So I got a job near the Little North Railroad. When I heard that notice on the radio, I came down here as fast as I could. I rode all night. I haven't had a happy moment since Chi-Chi died. Who was kind enough to put that news on the radio?"

"Grandfather," said four voices.

"Thank you, Grandfather," said the Thin Man with a bow. Everybody laughed.

Just then Mr. Carr said, "I am sorry to stop this party, but the train has to go along."

"Could I go, too?" asked the Thin Man. "I want to stop and see my friend Old Beaver. It will save me a lot of time if you could take me and my motorcycle on board."

Mr. Carr laughed. He said, "We're not supposed to stop at Beaver Lake. But I guess we can stop long enough to let you off."

The Aldens went up the steps of Number 777. The Thin Man followed with his motorcycle. Then the train moved away, leaving behind some good friends who were still laughing and pointing and waving.

CHAPTER 14

Best Trip of All

The train did stop at Beaver Lake after all. On the way from Pinedale, Benny said, "I'm glad you're going to see Old Beaver. He has been angry ever since the police made you run away."

"Yes, he would be," said the Thin Man. "He didn't know a thing about the money sewed in my coat. But he knew I'd never steal anything. By the way, where did you find the diamonds?"

"In the old black mattress in the lookout," said Henry.

"Oh," said the Thin Man, thinking it over. He nodded. "Yes, Chi-Chi did sleep there once in a while. You see the owner's wife was important. She always slept in the lower bunk. But she thought a lot of Chi-Chi."

The train slowed down for Beaver Lake. The Thin Man was all ready to get off.

"Here I go," he said. "I'm going to see Old Beaver every week on my motorcycle. He is still my best friend."

The Aldens watched him take the motorcycle off, then the train started again.

Jessie said, "Well, I'm glad those two are together. We don't have to worry any more about either of them."

The train rattled along without stopping. But the Aldens had plenty to talk about. They talked about their new friends and all their adventures.

"You solved the mystery as usual, Ben," said Henry.

"Well, I don't know," said Benny. "Nobody could have solved it if Jessie hadn't mended my mattress."

Benny was quiet for a minute. Then he exclaimed, "Say! I just thought of something. Supposing we had told Grandfather's friend we wanted new mattress covers! We would never have found those diamonds!"

"Good for you, Ben," said Henry. "And nobody else would have, either."

Mr. Alden agreed. "I think they would have been covered up for good. And now I think I shall begin to pack."

"I don't really want to pack," said Benny. "I could go on and on riding in this caboose forever."

"Well, I couldn't," said Mr. Alden. "I have to get back to work. I shall fly to New York and sell the necklace the very first thing I do."

The next morning, the train began to slow down for the last stop. It ran into the freightyard where the Aldens had started on their caboose adventure. They were all on the back platform, ready to get out. The train stopped.

Benny shouted, "Yes, John Carter has come to meet us. The station wagon is right over there."

Mr. John Carter worked for Grandfather in a great many ways. Everyone called, "Hello, Mr.

Carter!" as they stepped off the caboose.

"I'm glad to see you back," he called back. "And somebody else is glad, too. Here he is!"

Mr. Carter opened the car door, and Watch jumped out. He dashed over to Jessie. Then he went from one to another, barking and jumping. They each gave him a pat as he dashed on to the next one.

Benny said, "Watch, your name ought to be Dash. I didn't know how fast you could run around. And I didn't know how glad I'd be to see you."

All the railroad men began to help take the things out of the caboose. Mr. Carter and Henry packed them in the Alden car.

Al said, "Maybe you will go again sometime. You were wonderful passengers."

Mr. Carr said, "It was a pleasure to have you aboard."

"I was just going to say that," said Mr. Davis. "It was exciting, too!"

The Aldens piled into the station wagon and waved until the men were out of sight. When Henry drove the car up to the front door, they all unpacked the car. Mr. Alden went in and started to open his mail.

He called, "This is for all of us. It's a postcard from Charley. He says how much he uses his knife."

"Let me see it," said Benny. "Yes, that's a picture of the old station at Glass Factory. I'll never forget that place."

In a little while the Aldens sat down to supper.

"I think I'll pack some clean things," said Grandfather, "and fly to New York tomorrow."

"Tomorrow!" said Jessie. "You just got home!"

"I know," said Mr. Alden. "But I want to sell that necklace and send the money to Cho-Cho."

"I don't blame you, Grandfather," said Henry. "You'd like to get it off your mind."

Grandfather returned the same day from his trip.

"Oh, I'm so glad I went," he told them. "A jeweler bought the diamonds for a good price. But he paid twice as much as I expected for the ruby. He said it was especially fine, and he could easily sell it." Grandfather smiled at the thought. "So Cho-Cho's worries are over."

A week later a real letter came from Cho-Cho himself. Inside was a picture of Cho-Cho sitting in the cab of a truck. A horse-trailer with a roof was behind the truck. There was Major looking out of the big window.

"There's Major's little house," said Benny. "I was hoping he would have a roof over his head when it rains. I'd like to go South with them, Jessie."

"I think we have traveled enough for a while," said Jessie. "But didn't we have a grand time!"

"I think the caboose was the best adventure we ever had," said Violet.

They all agreed.

And if the Little North Railroad could talk, it would have said, "This is the very best trip I ever had in my whole life, even when I used to carry the gold-and-white circus caboose, Number 777."